Disney PRESENTS A PIXAR FILM
THE INCREDIBLES

ADVANCE PUBLISHERS

Published by Advance Publishers, L.C.
Maitland, FL 32751 USA
www.advancepublishers.com
Produced by Judy O Productions, Inc.
Designed by SunDried Penguin
© 2006 Disney Enterprises, Inc./Pixar Animation Studios
The Incredibles
The term"Omnidroid" used by permission of Lucasfilm Ltd.
Printed in the United States of America

During the golden age of Supers, one hero stood above the rest. His name was Mr Incredible – he was so strong, he could capture the world's worst villains. There were other Supers, too. Frozone could freeze bad guys in their tracks; Gazerbeam had laser-like vision; and Elastigirl (who later married Mr Incredible), could stretch whole streets to catch villains.

Everyone loved the Supers, but a boy named Buddy was Mr Incredible's biggest fan. He even called himself Incrediboy and invented a pair of rocket boots to help him fly. But Supers were born – not made. One day, Buddy really wanted to help Mr Incredible capture a thief, but Mr Incredible said, "Fly home Buddy. I work alone." Buddy felt rejected by his hero ...

The golden age of Supers came to a sudden end when too many lawsuits and complaints piled up against the Supers. The Super Relocation Program was created – the heroes were given new identities and told not to use their powers. Mr Incredible became Bob Parr, an insurance clerk. Elastigirl became Helen Parr, still Bob's wife and mom to their three kids. The kids had Super powers, too – Dash had Super speed and Violet could become invisible and create force fields. Only baby Jack-Jack seemed to have no powers. But the Parr family had to keep their powers a secret.

One night, Lucius Best – otherwise known as Frozone – came to visit. Bob and Lucius pretended to go bowling, but they were really listening to a police radio in their car, hoping to do hero work. They heard of a building fire and rushed to help save the people inside. But they didn't notice a mysterious woman watching them from the shadows. When Bob got home, Helen saw rubble on his shoulder and knew Bob was doing hero work again.

At his insurance office the next day, Bob got fired for helping clients. When he got home, he found a tiny computer hidden inside his briefcase. "Hello, Mr Incredible," said the woman on the screen. "My name is Mirage. We have need of your unique abilities. If you accept, your payment will be three times your current annual salary." Mr Incredible couldn't resist. He didn't want to tell Helen he'd lost his job, so he told her he had to go out of town for work.

The next morning, he secretly dressed in his old Super suit – a bit of a tight squeeze! – and met with Mirage on a jet headed for the island of Nomanisan. On the jet, Mirage told Mr Incredible his mission was to find and shut down the Omnidroid, a top-secret battle robot. Soon after they landed, the Omnidroid found Mr Incredible. After a fight, Mr Incredible beat the robot. Unknown to him, Mirage was watching everything with a mysterious man …

After Bob returned home, Mirage called him back to Nomanisan. On the island, Mr Incredible was surprised he recognized the mysterious man – it was Buddy! "I am Syndrome! Your nemesis!" he screamed. Buddy had invented the Omnidroid to defeat the Supers because he was angry with Mr Incredible for not letting him help all those years ago. He slammed Mr Incredible off a cliff, but the hero survived and hid in an underwater cave.

Back at home, Helen visited Super designer Edna Mode (otherwise known as E). When Helen saw the new Super suits E had designed for Bob and their whole family, she knew he was working as a Super again. Helen pushed the homing device on Bob's new suit to find out where he'd gone ... Meanwhile, back on Nomanisan, Mr Incredible discovered that Syndrome's plan was to kill off the Supers and launch his remote control Omnidroid to take over the city. Then he would defeat the Omnidroid and become the world's top Super. Suddenly Mr Incredible's homing device beeped and he was trapped!

Helen rushed to the island to find her husband. Elastigirl was ready for action! And so were Dash and Vi – they had stowed away on the plane, leaving Jack-Jack at home with a babysitter! When they reached the island, Elastigirl told the kids to wait while she went to find their father. "If anything goes wrong, use your Super powers," she told them.

Elastigirl raced through the jungle to Syndrome's headquarters and found Mr Incredible with Mirage. Mirage told the Incredibles that Dash and Vi were in trouble, so they took off to rescue their children. But just as Mr Incredible and Elastigirl saved Dash and Vi from the island guards, Syndrome turned up! He suspended the whole family in mid-air with his immobi-rays, then left to release his Omnidroid on Metroville.

Luckily, Vi had used her force field Super powers and she was able to free her family. The Incredibles returned to Metroville just in time to see Syndrome defeated and send the Omnidroid to its doom. When they got to their house, though, Syndrome was there and he had baby Jack-Jack. But Jack-Jack was an Incredible after all and he turned into a howling mini-monster. Terrified, Syndrome let Jack-Jack go, just as Mr Incredible threw a car at Syndrome, who was about to escape in his hover jet. The jet exploded and Syndrome was defeated!

Soon, the Incredibles returned
to their undercover life,
and everything was
back to normal. Well sort of …

The End